The farm is tiny. The coop is itsy-bitsy. The chickens are very small. But the egg is humongous, and so is the huge yellow fellow who pops out! This feathered giant is so big, the flock is sure he's no chicken.

The big guy has an equally big heart, however, and longs to be accepted as one of the chickens. Little by little, his kindness and brave rescue of the flock's eggs prove to the silly chickens that he is really one of them.

I think it's an elephant.

I've never seen anything so big!

I think we should run for our lives!

"Graves has great fun . . . preserving the message that fools jump to hasty conclusions—and kids will, too."
—*Publishers Weekly*

"For all kids who know they are really smarter than the grown-ups." —*Kirkus Reviews*

"An amusing tale that will draw giggles from preschool and early elementary read-aloud audiences, this is a fun addition to any collection or comparative folklore unit." —*School Library Journal*

An E.B. White Read Aloud Award Honor Book
A BookPage Best Children's Book

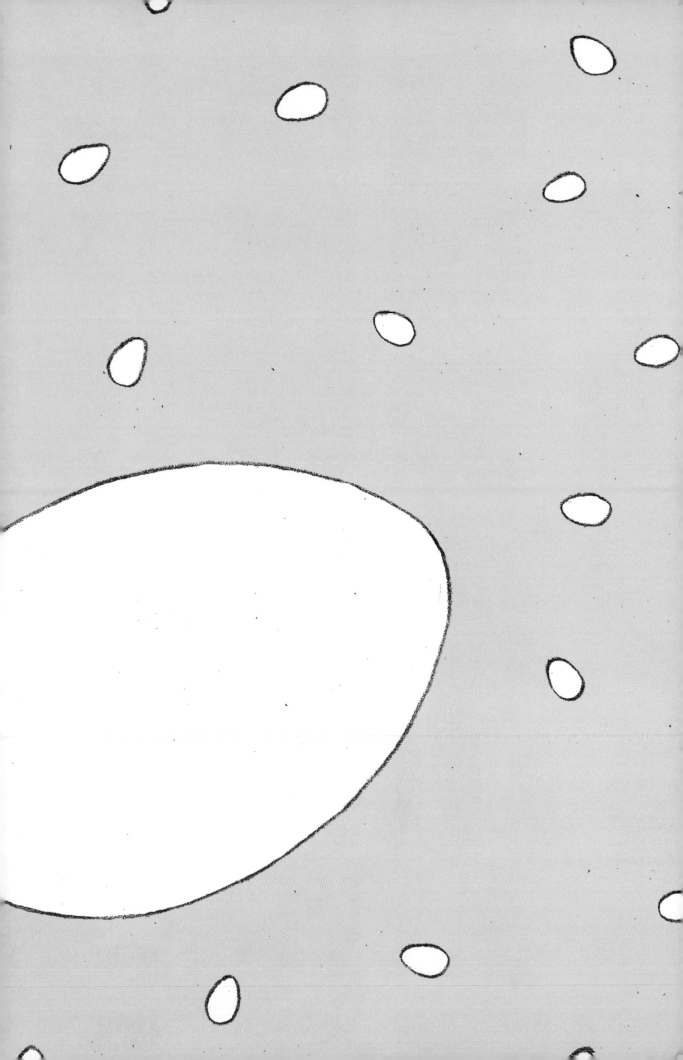

What should we call this book?
How about Chicken Kind of Large!
OR...Chicken Tall!
No, no, no. CHICKEN SALAD!

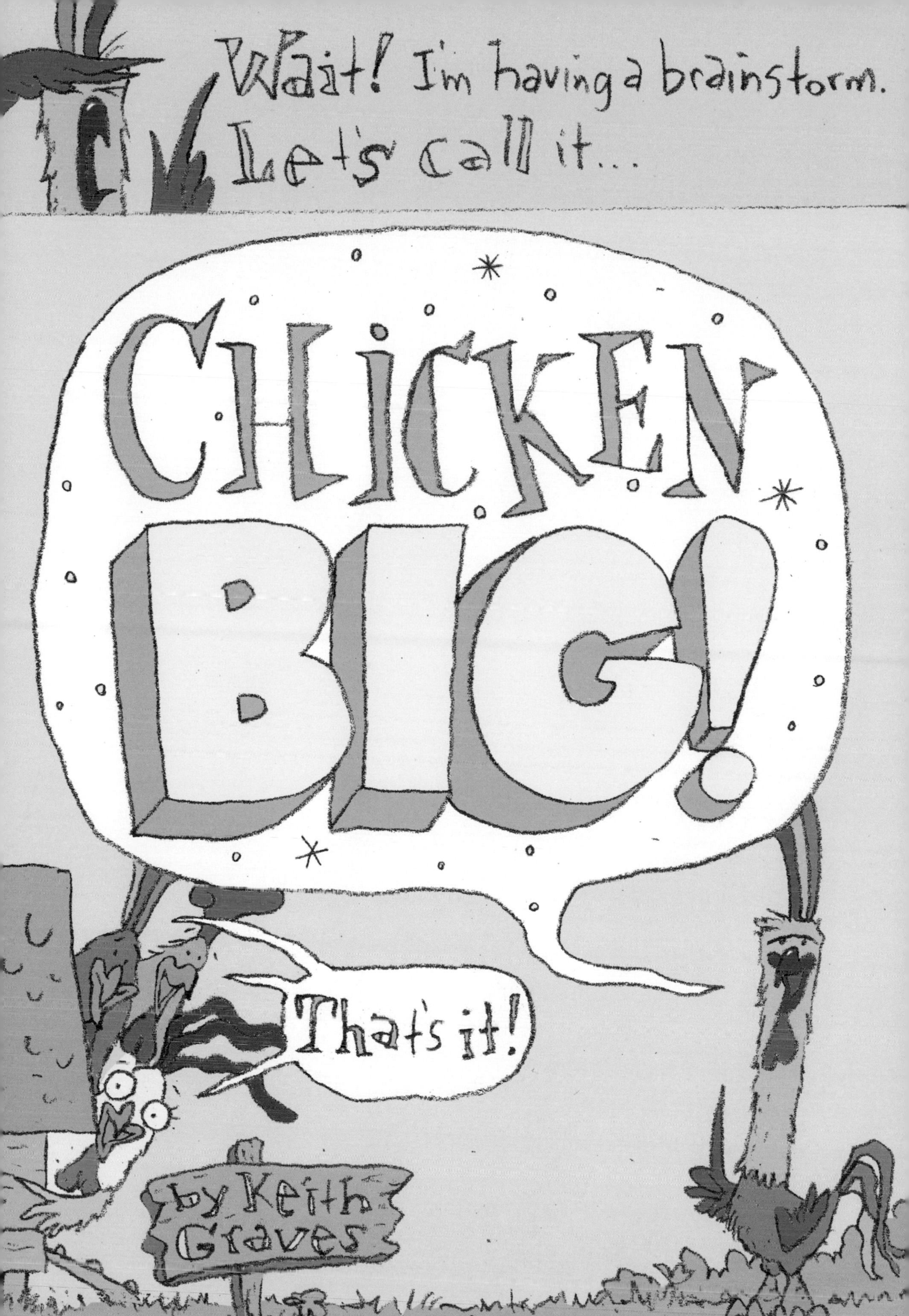

chronicle books · san francisco

On a teeny little farm,

in an itty-bitty coop,

a very small hen laid a big, humongous egg.

Bok!

The egg began to shake.
The egg began to quake.

Out popped a big, humongous chick.

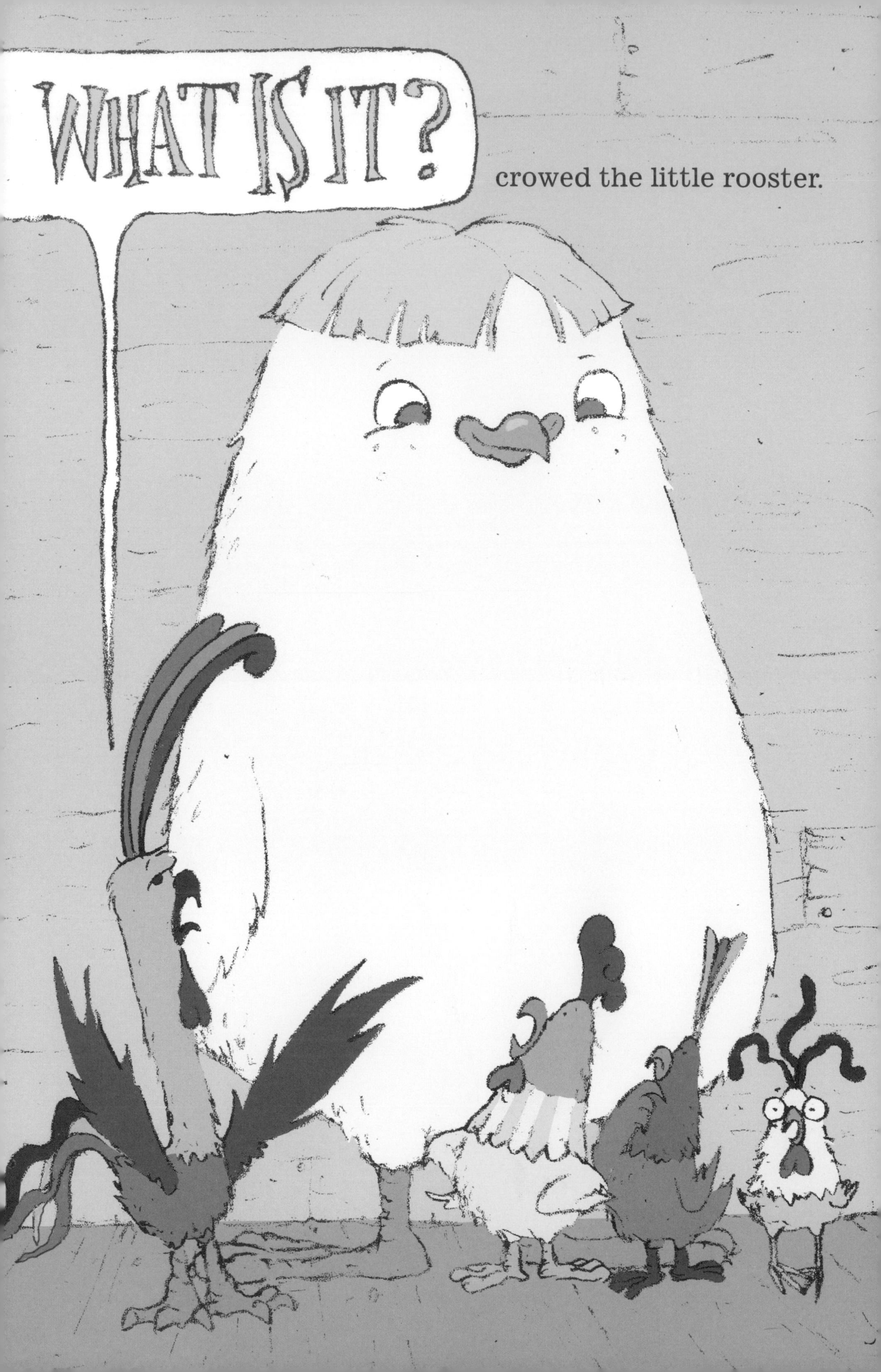

crowed the little rooster.

"It's big!" clucked the small chicken.

"It's enormous!" clucked the smaller chicken.

"It's an *elephant!*" peeped the smallest chicken.

(She was not the sharpest beak in the flock.)

"He's too big to stay in our itty-bitty coop," crowed the little rooster.

"Much, much too big," clucked the small chicken.

"He'll break the floor!" clucked the smaller chicken.

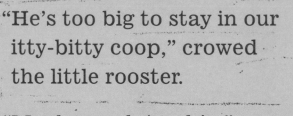

INDOOR ELEPHANTS ARE DANGEROUS!

squawked the smallest chicken.

"I don't feel like an elephant," thought the big chick.

The next day,

an acorn fell and conked the
smallest chicken on the head.

"The sky is falling!" she peeped.
"Run for your lives!"

CLOCK!

So, the chickens ran for their lives.

"Don't worry," said the big, humongous chick. It's only an acorn. They're actually quite tasty."

"I don't think elephants eat acorns,"
said the little rooster.

"I heard they only eat popcorn,"
clucked the small chicken.

"Maybe he's not an elephant,"
clucked the smaller chicken.

The smallest chicken looked closely
at the big, humongous chick.

"Ah, my mistake," she peeped.

He must be a SQUIRREL!

"A squirrel?" thought the big humongous chick.

Later on, the smallest chicken was pecking for worms when a raindrop splatted on top of her head.

"The sky is leaking!" she peeped. "We'll all drown! Run for your lives!"

And the chickens ran for their lives again.

"Relax," said the big, humongous chick.

"It's only rain. Come stand under my wings and you will stay dry."

"I've never seen a squirrel do that," crowed the little rooster.

"Not very squirrel-ish at all," clucked the small chicken.

"Squirrels don't keep you dry in the rain," clucked the smaller chicken.

"I see what you're saying," peeped the smallest chicken.

Apparently, he is an UMBRELLA!

"These are not bright chickens," thought the big chick.

After a while,
a chilly wind began to blow.

"Someone has put the world in the refrigerator!" peeped the smallest chicken. "We're all going to freeze!"

"RUN FOR YOUR LIVES!"

But they didn't get far.

"Don't panic," said the big, humongous chick.

"It is only the north wind. Stand behind me and I will protect you."

The chickens all felt much better.

"An umbrella would have turned inside out in this wind," crowed the little rooster.

"He's not inside out as far as I can tell," clucked the small chicken.

"I'm all warm and comfy now," clucked the smaller chicken.

"Only one thing makes me feel this way," peeped the smallest chicken.

"Plainly, this fellow is . . .

A SWEATER!

"This is getting ridiculous,"
thought the big,
humongous chick.

At naptime, the little chickens returned to the coop and found all their eggs were gone.

"We've been robbed!" crowed the little rooster.

"By an egg burglar!" clucked the small chicken.

"Woe is me!" clucked the smaller chicken.

"Woe is me, too!" peeped the smallest chicken.

The chickens all began to boo hoo hoo.

But the big, humongous chick saw
a sneaky red fox carrying the eggs
into his den a mile away.

With three giant hop-hop-hops, the big, humongous chick caught up to the fox just as he was about to make himself a scrambled egg supper.

"Yikes!" said the fox.

"I don't think so," said the big, humongous chick. "But you are a naughty thief!"

The frightened fox ran away with his tail between his legs, having lost all interest in poultry.

In no time, the big chick was stomping back to the coop with the missing eggs.

"Our babies!" cried the happy, little chickens.

"Our hero!" they all clucked.

"I knew it all along!" crowed the little rooster. "He's no elephant!"

"He's definitely not a squirrel!" clucked the small chicken.

"He's surely no umbrella!" clucked the smaller chicken.

"He couldn't be a sweater!" peeped the smallest chicken.

"Only ONE thing could be so smart, so kind, so warm, and so brave."

The big, humongous chick was THRILLED to find out that he was a chicken after all.

"Oh thank goodness!" he said. "Now I can move back into the coop!"

"Actually, it's a rather small coop," crowed the little rooster.

"It's itty-bitty," clucked the small chicken.

"Teensy-weensy," clucked the smaller chicken.

But we'll make room!

peeped the smallest chicken.

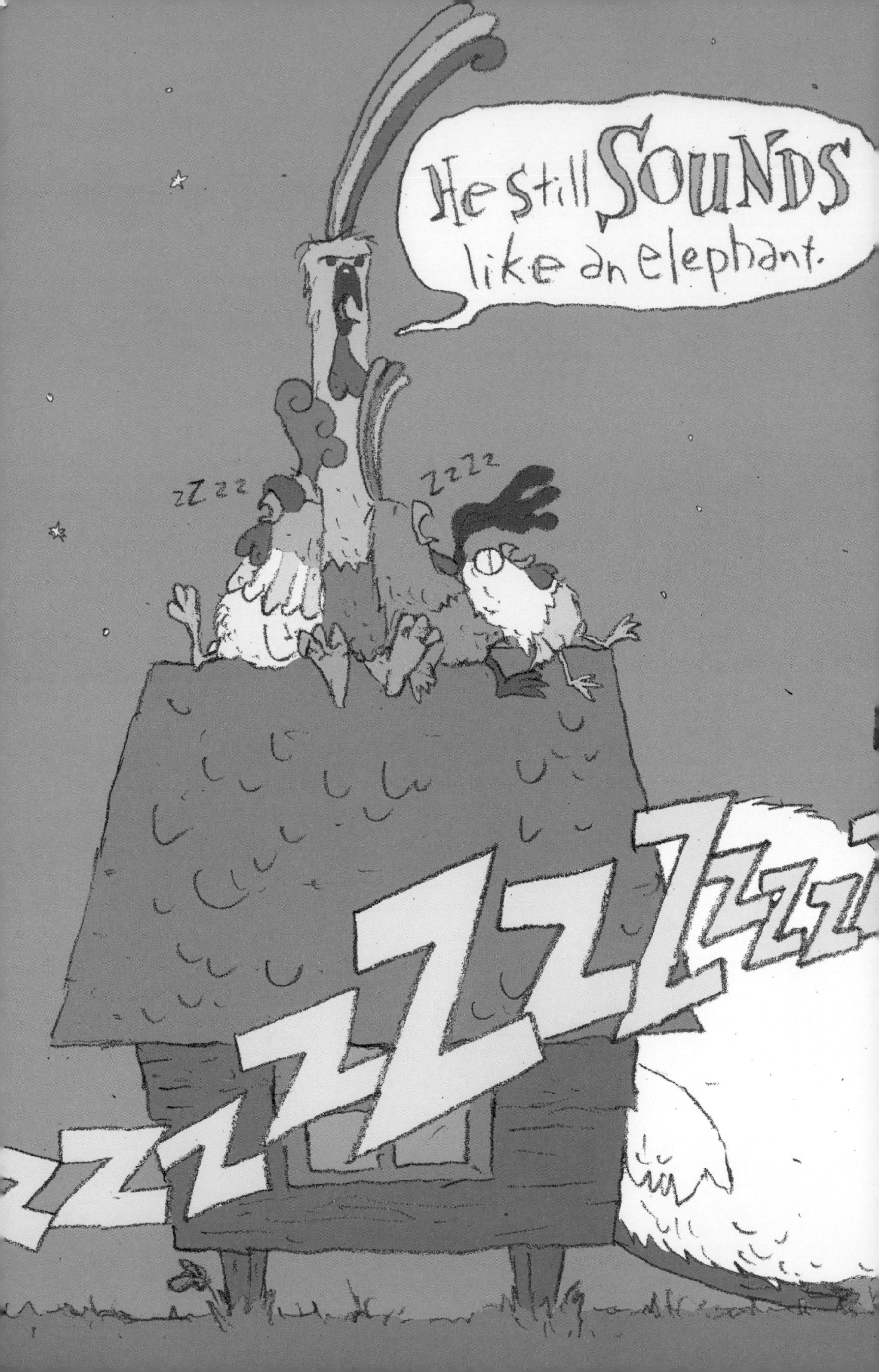
He still SOUNDS like an elephant.
ZZZZ
ZZZZ
ZZZZZZZZZZ

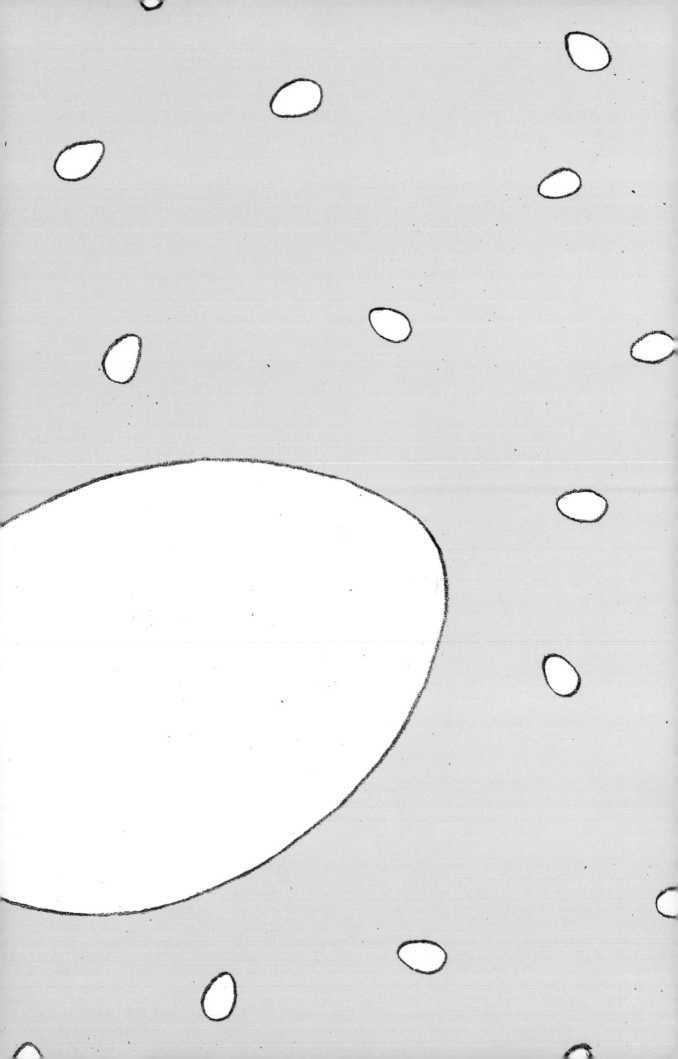

Keith Graves is Professor Emeritus at the Chicken School in Austin, Texas, where he teaches courses in chicken psychology and chicken history. Strangely, Professor Graves has the exact same name as another guy who wrote the book *Frank Was a Monster Who Wanted to Dance*, as well as some other ridiculous books, but we doubt he's the same guy.

First paperback edition published in 2014 by Chronicle Books LLC.
Originally published in hardcover in 2010 by Chronicle Books LLC.
Copyright © 2010 by Keith Graves.
All rights reserved. No part of this book may be reproduced in any form without written permission from the publisher.

ISBN 978-1-4521-3146-7

The Library of Congress has cataloged the original edition as follows:
Graves, Keith.
  Chicken Big / by Keith Graves.
     p. cm.
  Summary: A giant chicken hatches from an enormous egg, but the other chickens cannot accept that he is one of them.
  ISBN 978-0-8118-7237-9 (alk. paper)
  [1. Chickens—Fiction. 2. Size—Fiction. 3. Humorous stories.] I. Title.
  PZ7.G77524Ch 2010
  [E]—dc22
  2009048560

Manufactured in China.

Design by Rachel Liang.
Typeset in News 701.
The illustrations in this book were rendered in chicken scratch (pencil and pixels).

10 9 8 7 6

Chronicle Books LLC
680 Second Street
San Francisco, California 94107

Chronicle Books—we see things differently.
Become part of our community at www.chroniclekids.com.